Put Beginning Readers on the Right Track with
ALL ABOARD READING™

The All Aboard Reading series is especially designed for beginning readers. Written by noted authors and illustrated in full color, these are books that children really want to read—books to excite their imagination, expand their interests, make them laugh, and support their feelings. With fiction and nonfiction stories that are high interest and curriculum-related, All Aboard Reading books offer something for every young reader. And with four different reading levels, the All Aboard Reading series lets you choose which books are most appropriate for your children and their growing abilities.

Picture Readers
Picture Readers have super-simple texts, with many nouns appearing as rebus pictures. At the end of each book are 24 flash cards—on one side is a rebus picture; on the other side is the written-out word.

Station Stop 1
Station Stop 1 books are best for children who have just begun to read. Simple words and big type make these early reading experiences more comfortable. Picture clues help children to figure out the words on the page. Lots of repetition throughout the text helps children to predict the next word or phrase—an essential step in developing word recognition.

Station Stop 2
Station Stop 2 books are written specifically for children who are reading with help. Short sentences make it easier for early readers to understand what they are reading. Simple plots and simple dialogue help children with reading comprehension.

Station Stop 3
Station Stop 3 books are perfect for children who are reading alone. With longer text and harder words, these books appeal to children who have mastered basic reading skills. More complex stories captivate children who are ready for more challenging books.

In addition to All Aboard Reading books, look for All Aboard Math Readers™ (fiction stories that teach math concepts children are learning in school); All Aboard Science Readers™ (nonfiction books that explore the most fascinating science topics in age-appropriate language); All Aboard Poetry Readers™ (funny, rhyming poems for readers of all levels); and All Aboard Mystery Readers™ (puzzling tales where children piece together evidence with the characters).

All Aboard for happy reading!

For my mother, Esther Hautzig—Deborah Hautzig
To Grandma Dede, who shared her lovely books
with me—Kathryn Rathke

GROSSET & DUNLAP
Published by the Penguin Group
Penguin Group (USA) Inc., 375 Hudson Street, New York, New York 10014, USA
Penguin Group (Canada), 90 Eglinton Avenue East, Suite 700, Toronto, Ontario M4P 2Y3, Canada
(a division of Pearson Penguin Canada Inc.)
Penguin Books Ltd., 80 Strand, London WC2R 0RL, England
Penguin Group Ireland, 25 St. Stephen's Green, Dublin 2, Ireland
(a division of Penguin Books Ltd.)
Penguin Group (Australia), 250 Camberwell Road, Camberwell, Victoria 3124, Australia
(a division of Pearson Australia Group Pty. Ltd.)
Penguin Books India Pvt. Ltd., 11 Community Centre, Panchsheel Park, New Delhi—110 017, India
Penguin Group (NZ), 67 Apollo Drive, Rosedale, North Shore 0632, New Zealand
(a division of Pearson New Zealand Ltd.)
Penguin Books (South Africa) (Pty.) Ltd., 24 Sturdee Avenue,
Rosebank, Johannesburg 2196, South Africa

Penguin Books Ltd., Registered Offices: 80 Strand, London WC2R 0RL, England

Library of Congress Control Number: 2009015707

ISBN 978-0-448-45269-2   10 9 8 7 6 5 4 3 2 1

Lewis Carroll's

Alice in Wonderland

Adapted by Deborah Hautzig
Illustrated by Kathryn Rathke

Grosset & Dunlap
An Imprint of Penguin Group (USA) Inc.

One hot summer day, Alice was lying
down by the river with her sister. She felt
very bored and sleepy.

Suddenly, a white rabbit ran past her.

Alice was amazed to see that the White Rabbit was holding a watch! He looked at it and said, "Oh no! I am late!"

Alice followed him as he ran off. He popped down a rabbit hole, and Alice went right down after him.

Alice fell down, down, down the rabbit hole. She passed bookshelves, jars of jam, and maps.

"I wonder how many miles I have fallen?" Alice asked aloud. "I wish my cat, Dinah, were here with me!"

Thump! Alice landed on a pile of leaves.

She saw the White Rabbit running down a long hall and she chased after him. But he turned a corner and disappeared.

There were doors all around the hall.
Each of them was locked.

Alice noticed that one door was the size
of a rat hole. Then she saw a tiny golden key
on a glass table.

She took the key, kneeled down, and unlocked the tiny door. Through the doorway, she could see a beautiful garden.

"Oh, I wish I could go in!" said Alice.

But, of course, she was much too big. So she locked the door and stood up.

When Alice put the key back on the
table, she noticed a bottle. It had not been
there before. The label read: DRINK ME.

"What if it is poison?" she asked wisely.

But the label did not say "poison," so she
tasted it.

"Mmm! Cherry pie and roast turkey!"
said Alice. Then she drank it all up.

Suddenly, Alice began to shrink! Soon, she was just the right size to go through the tiny door and into the garden. But the door was locked and Alice was too small to reach the key up on the table! Poor Alice cried and cried.

As Alice wiped her tears, she noticed
a tiny piece of cake. It was in a glass box
under the table. There were two words on
the cake: EAT ME.

"Maybe this will help," said Alice as she
took a bite.

Alice began to grow bigger. She grew and grew until she was nine feet tall!

Now Alice could easily reach the key, but she was too big to fit through the tiny door. Alice began to cry again. This time, her tears were so huge that they made a pool of water.

Suddenly, the White Rabbit came
hurrying past. He was holding a white fan.
"I'm late! I'm late!" said the White
Rabbit.
"Please," cried Alice. "Can you help me?"

The White Rabbit was so startled that he dropped his fan. Then he ran off as quickly as he could.

"Now what?" asked Alice with a sigh. She picked up the fan and began fanning herself.

Before long, she was small again.

"How did that happen?" she wondered. Then she saw that the more she fanned herself, the smaller she became! As she quickly dropped the fan, she slipped and fell into the deep pool of tears.

Alice saw a mouse splashing about in the water, and she swam over to it.

"Oh, Mouse, do you know the way out of this pool?"

"Shore is that way!" answered the Mouse. He pointed straight ahead.

Soon Alice reached the shore. There she saw a blue caterpillar sitting on a mushroom.

"Who are you?" asked the Caterpillar.

"I thought I was a little girl," said Alice. "But I keep changing! It's so confusing."

"No, it's not," said the Caterpillar.

"It is to me," said Alice.

"Here, have some of my mushroom," said the Caterpillar. "One side makes you big, the other small."

Alice nibbled on the mushroom until she was back to her normal size. Then she put some of the mushroom in her pocket for later.

"Thank you," she said politely. But the Caterpillar had already disappeared.

"Which way do I go from here?" asked Alice aloud.

"That depends on where you want to go!" said a voice from above.

Alice looked up and saw a cat sitting on a tree branch. It was grinning from ear to ear.

"I didn't know cats could grin," said Alice. "My cat, Dinah, never grins."

"I am a Cheshire cat. We always grin," said the Cat.

"What sort of people live here?" asked Alice as she looked up at the Cat.

The Cat pointed and said, "A Hatter lives that way. A March Hare lives this way. You can visit either. But both are mad."

"Oh dear," said Alice. "I don't want to meet mad people!"

"You can't help that. Everyone here is mad!" said the Cat. Then, bit by bit, the Cat started to disappear. Finally, all that was left was the Cat's big grin.

"I've seen many cats without grins, but never a grin without a cat," said Alice. And off she went.

Soon, Alice came to the Mad Hatter's house. The Hatter and the March Hare were having a tea party. There was a Dormouse who was fast asleep.

They were all crowded into one corner of a long table. Alice went to sit down.

"No room! No room!" they said to Alice.

"Nonsense," said Alice, taking a seat.
"There is plenty of room!"

"Have more tea," said the Hatter.

"But I haven't had any yet. I can't take
more," said Alice.

"You mean you can't take *less*!" said the
Hare.

Alice was very confused.

"I have a riddle for you," said the Hatter.

"Oh, I love riddles!" said Alice.

"Why is a raven like a writing desk?" he asked.

Alice thought and thought.

"I give up," she said at last. "What's the answer?"

"I have no idea!" said the Hatter.

Alice stood up and said, "This is the worst tea party ever!" Then she stomped off into the woods.

Alice stopped at a tree with a door in its trunk.

"How curious!" she said as she stepped inside. Now she was back in the hall with the tiny door. The golden key was still on the glass table. Alice picked it up and unlocked the little door.

Then she nibbled on the mushroom that was in her pocket. Alice began to shrink! Soon, she was just the right size to enter the garden.

The garden was filled with flowers, trees, and fountains.

There were also two very strange gardeners. Their bodies looked just like playing cards! And they were painting white roses red.

"Excuse me," said Alice. "Why are you painting those roses?"

"The Queen wants only red roses," said one gardener. "If they are white, she will cut off our heads."

"Uh-oh!" called the other gardener.
"Here come the King and Queen of Hearts.
Their soldiers are coming, too!"

The soldiers looked just like the
gardeners.

The Queen was very angry when she saw that some of the roses were still white. She pointed at the gardeners and screamed, "Off with their heads!"

But then the Queen saw Alice and forgot about the gardeners.

"Who are you?" shouted the Queen.

"I am Alice, your Majesty," she answered.

"Can you play croquet?" asked the Queen.

"Yes, of course," said Alice.

"Then let's play!" yelled the Queen.

The balls were live hedgehogs. The mallets were flamingos. Alice had a hard time playing. The ball wouldn't stay still, and the flamingo kept twisting its long neck to stare at her! Alice couldn't help but laugh.

Alice had never played croquet like this before. And strangest of all, the Queen kept screaming, "Off with their heads!"

Then someone called out, "The trial is about to start!"

"What trial?" wondered Alice aloud.

Alice went to the court. The Queen and King were on their thrones. The White Rabbit was there, too. There was a large dish of tarts on a table in front of them.

The King asked, "What is the crime?"

The White Rabbit blew his trumpet. Then he read from a scroll, "The Jack of Hearts stole the tarts!"

"Call the first witness!" said the King.

"The Mad Hatter," the White Rabbit read.

"I don't know anything," said the Hatter.

He was so scared, he was shaking.

"Dismissed!" said the King. "Next witness!" shouted the King.

"Alice," called the White Rabbit.

Alice was so surprised!

"Here I am, your Majesty," she said.

"Well? What do you know?" asked the King.

"I know this trial makes no sense," said Alice. "The tarts are right there on the table. They were never stolen after all!"

"Case dismissed," said the King.

"NO!" screamed the Queen. "We must punish the Jack of Hearts."

"But that's nonsense," said Alice. "You can't punish him if there wasn't a crime."

"Off with her head!" yelled the Queen, pointing at Alice.

The soldiers marched toward Alice. Then Alice shouted at the Queen, "This is the silliest trial I ever saw! I'm not afraid of you or your soldiers. They are just a pack of cards!"

The soldiers were furious! All of them rose up into the air. Alice screamed as the cards came flying at her.

Alice waved her arms to push the cards away and found herself on a riverbank. Her sister gently brushed away some dead leaves that had fallen on Alice's face.

"Wake up, Alice, dear," said Alice's sister. "You've had such a long nap!"

Alice rubbed her eyes and said, "Oh, what a strange dream I had!"

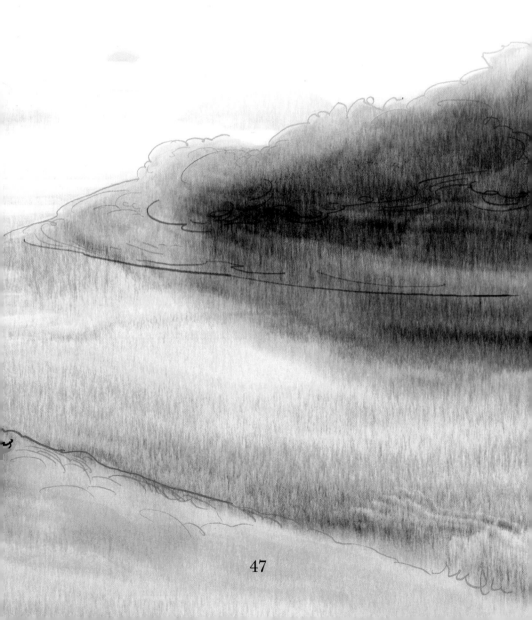

Alice told her sister all about her adventures. She told her about the White Rabbit, the Mad Hatter, the Cheshire Cat, and everyone else she had met.

"That *was* a strange dream!" said her sister. "Now run home. It's late, and Dinah will be wanting her bowl of milk."

So off Alice ran, thinking what a wonderful dream it had been.